per, fly a triplane, find **Planet Doughnut**,

ool, find a pelisnake, have green horned

v jelly, sit with an astronaut, visit Planet

space bus, drive a **shark motor boat**, eat

entipede, have **orange** and **blue hair**, find

ellow smoothie, eat **space crickets**, sit in

find a **furtle**, meet a **space troll** with big

ride a **space motorbike**, sleep in a spotty

d a zeep, eat **beans on blue toast**, fly with

stmas Pudding, visit the space bank, find a

th a **pink rabbit**, go to **Planet Glitter Ball**,

ar **starry tights**, go to the space cinema,

e maggots, find **Helter-Skelter Mountain**,

find a **shen**, swim in the space swimming

curl on his forehead, or slurp **blue soup**?

For Seven Stories, the National Centre for Children's Books – P.G. & N.S.

Seven Stories is Britain's home for children's literature and is proud
to care for Nick Sharratt's artwork in its acclaimed Collection.

PUFFIN BOOKS

UK | USA | Canada | Ireland | Australia
India | New Zealand | South Africa

Puffin Books is part of the Penguin Random House group of companies
whose addresses can be found at global.penguinrandomhouse.com.

www.penguin.co.uk   www.puffin.co.uk   www.ladybird.co.uk

Penguin
Random House
UK

First published 2017
This edition published 2018
001

Printed in China

A CIP catalogue record for this book is available from the British Library

ISBN: 978-0-141-37930-2

All correspondence to:
Puffin Books, Penguin Random House Children's,
80 Strand, London WC2R 0RL

FSC
www.fsc.org
MIX
Paper from
responsible sources
FSC® C018179

This book
belongs to:

Would you leap on a jet-propelled spacel
snooze in a rocking chair, go to space s
hair, collect space-rocket eggs, eat rainl
Orange, find an octo-owl, ride in a wob
pink eggs, go to the space museum, find
flying space dragons, drink a purple an
a floating pink and purple inflatable ch
blue ears, wear star glasses, eat blue mel
bunk bed, share popcorn with a queen,
Super Boy and Super Girl, go to Planet Cl
duckerfly, hop with a pangaroo, snooze
travel in a hover-train, eat blue curry,
find a crocoseal, chew a pink bone, eat l
wear a hat with fluffy ears, eat a red band
pool, make friends with the alien with

YOU
CHOOSE
IN SPACE

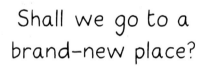

Shall we go to a
brand-new place?

Let's fly to a planet
out in space!

Look at the pictures
in this book and choose
your own space story.

Nick Sharratt & Pippa Goodhart

PUFFIN

We're off on an amazing trip.

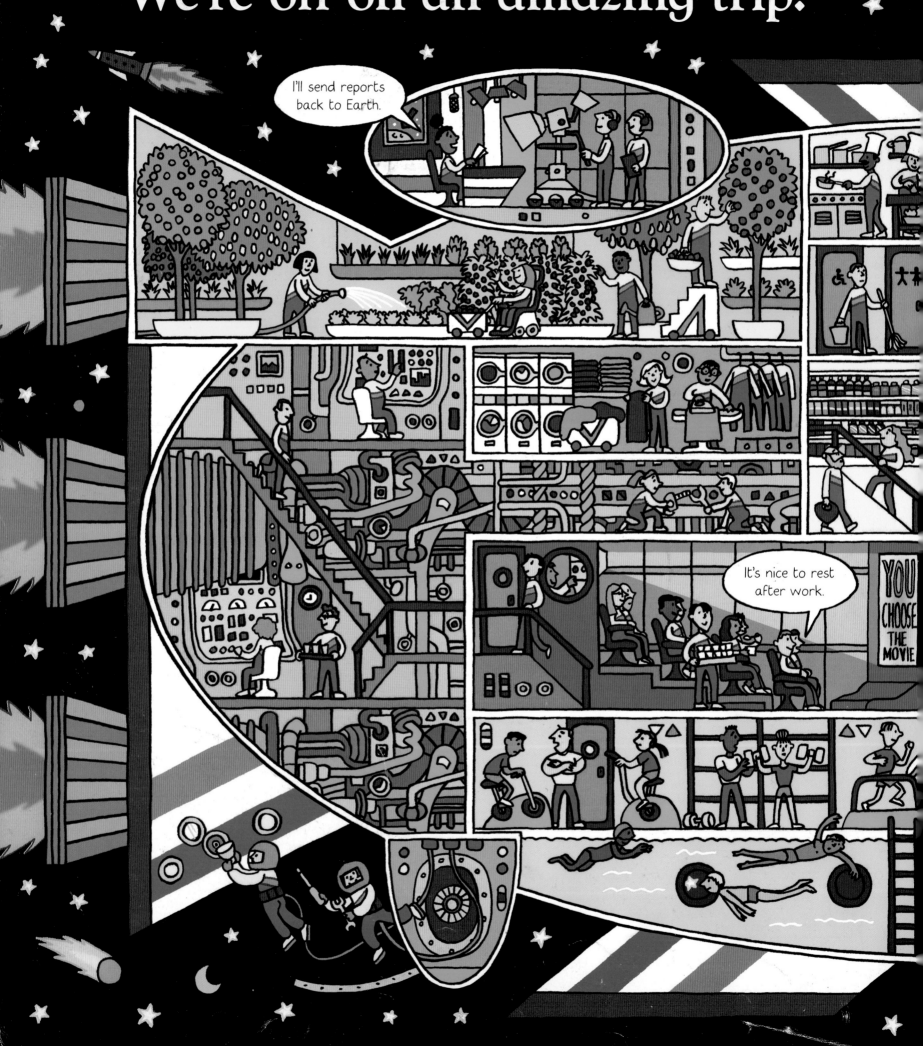

Choose a job aboard the ship.

While you're on this planet, you'll need new things to wear.

Choose some shoes and clothes, and how to style your hair.

Choose a friend.
What would you say?

Which one would you choose, and why?

Try new things to eat and drink.

Will they be nice? What do you think?

Let's go to the space show. Everyone's waiting for YOU!

It's your chance to be a star. What will YOU choose to do?

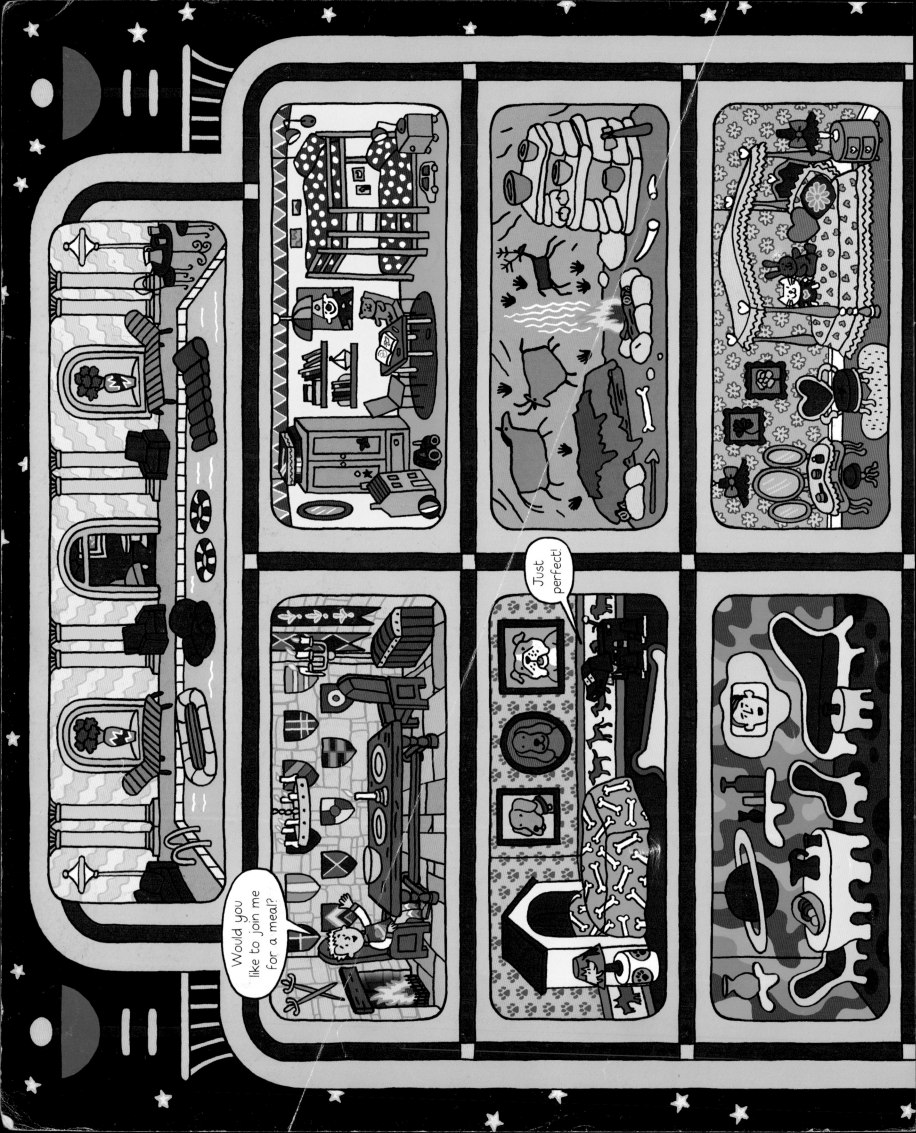

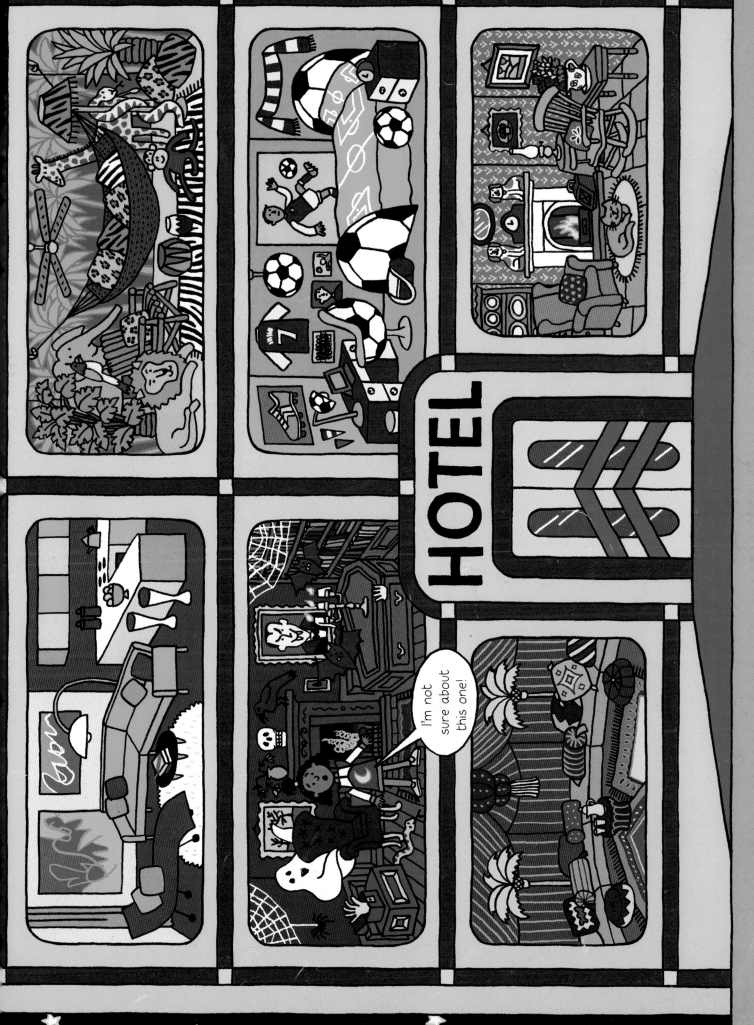

Time to rest — which room will you choose?
Settle in — and have a snooze.

ZOOM! We're off
into space once more.

Is it home time?
Or shall we explore?

Or would you go to Planet Square Sides, f
top, visit the space gallery, ride a blu
with a robot, spot a pog, eat purple
hover-sleigh, sit beside rude pixies, find
eat a bowl of dog food, find Triplosau
biscuits, touch fingers with a tall blue alie
wear your hair in a blue quiff, find fou
ostrabbit, slurp a smoothie with a ghost
queen, spot a dronkey, crunch a pink
a space big wheel, wear stripy trousers,
the space laundry, spot the space fire eng
pill, row a boat with red oars, find a ha
tickled by an owlopus, find two china
kebabs, spot a matching stripy jacket
orange hair, taste the silver space loll
zig-zag earrings, try stardust crisps, loo
play an alien guitar, spot a UFO, eat spo

crocodiles in purple water, wear a cactus
:ooter with a splog, eat an ice cream
:olate, sit in a football chair, fly in a
net Tennis Ball, spot a lucky black cat,
fossils, grow space flowers, bake alien
ithout a tail, find Pick-and-Mix Hospital,
untains squirting at once, hop with an
:ep on a pile of furs, eat popcorn with a
rot, run on a spaceship treadmill, ride
y three-decker noughts and crosses, do
, jump on a trampoline, eat an apple-pie
:oming out of a box, spot an eliorse, be
s on a mantelpiece, eat multi-coloured
. parasol, sleep in a bony bed, try tall
), fly up to Planet Drippy Blue, wear
t a dolphion, see two swords on a wall,
pink eggs, or wear a pair of pink shorts?

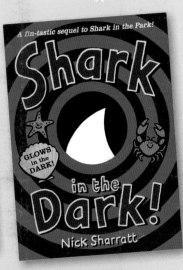

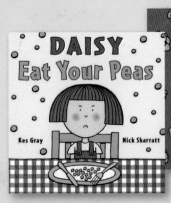

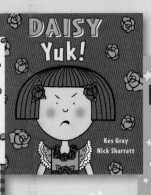

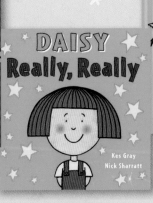

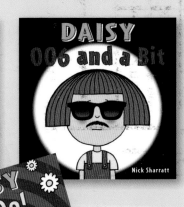

Why not choose
some more books
illustrated by Nick Sharratt?